What the Owl Saw

What the Owl Saw

DON CONROY

POOLBEG

FOR CHILDREN

Published 1998 by
Poolbeg Press Ltd
123 Baldoyle Industrial Estate
Dublin 13, Ireland

Text and illustrations © Don Conroy 1998

The moral right of the author has been asserted.

Reprinted October 1998

The Arts Council
An Chomhairle Ealaíon

A catalogue record for this book is available from the British Library.

ISBN 1 85371 863 7

Illustrations by Don Conroy
Cover design by Poolbeg Group Services Ltd
Set by Poolbeg Group Services Ltd in Times 15/22
Printed by The Guernsey Press Ltd,
Vale, Guernsey, Channel Islands.

Don's other books include:

The Anaconda from Drumcondra
Elephant at the Door
The Bookworm who Turned Over a New Leaf
*The Don Conroy Wildlife Colouring
and Activity Book*

To Aindriú

High in an old Scots pine tree lived a family of
long-eared owls. There was Mummy Owl and
Daddy Owl and two children, a boy and a girl.
The boy was called Hushy and the girl Coney.

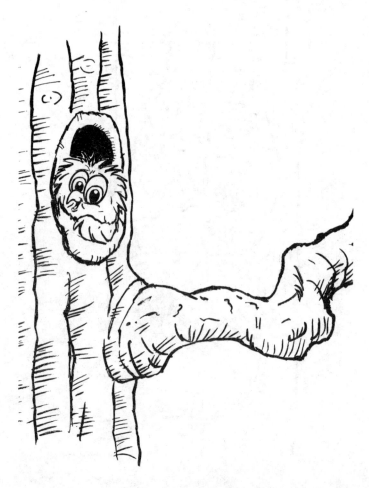

Hushy peered out of the hole in the tree. It looked so lovely outside he wondered should he climb out onto the large, thick branch and get an even better view of things.

He looked at his mummy and daddy to see if
they were awake. They didn't seem to be. In
fact, he could hear his daddy snoring loudly.
Even his sister, Coney, was fast asleep.

Very quietly Hushy sneaked out onto the branch. His mother blinked open one large orange eye. "Where do you think you are going?" she asked, as she watched him climb out of the nest.

"Oh, just outside, Mummy," said Hushy. "I want to see the world."

"Do be careful," said his mother. "And don't move from that branch."

"Oh, I won't, Mother dear."

Hushy watched his mother close her eyes again and go back to sleep.

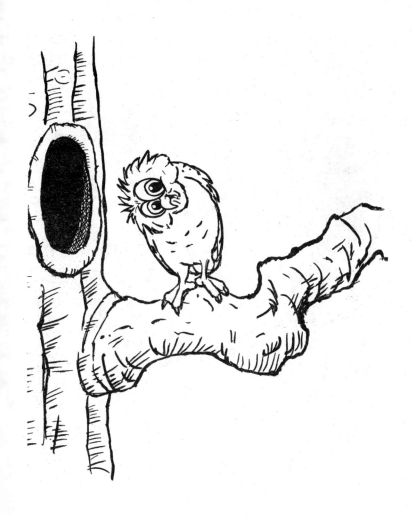

Hushy looked around the woods. Everything
was so beautiful.

There was a red disk just above the trees. It
made him blink.

"Mummy, Mummy, what's that red shape in the sky?"

"That's the sun, dear. You mustn't stare at it – it will hurt your eyes."

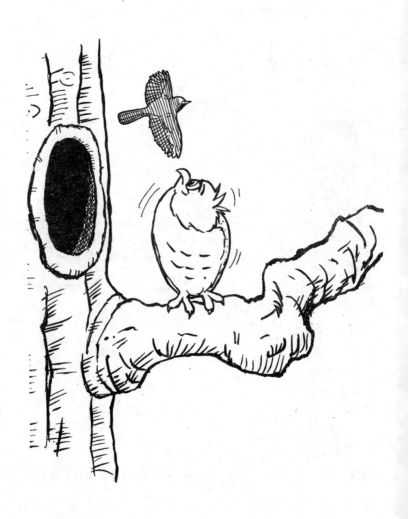

A robin flew close to Hushy and landed on a
small holly tree.

Then it sang a lovely song.

"Mummy, there is something else out here that has red on it. It sings, and it can fly."

"It's a robin, dear. Now will you be quiet! I'm trying to sleep."

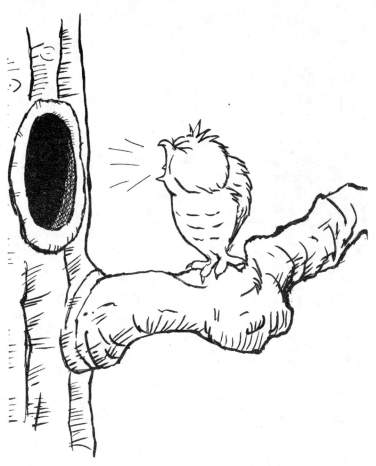

"OK, Mummy, I'll be very quiet."

"Oh, what a lovely day. I think I'll sing a song, just like that robin." Hushy took a deep breath and stretched his body. And gave out a loud shriek.

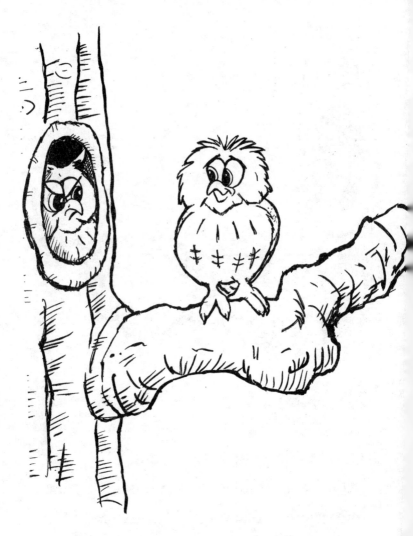

"What's all the noise?" asked his daddy, as he was awakened from a deep sleep.

"It's only me, Father dear. I'm trying to sing
like a robin."

"Owls don't sing," his father snapped.
"We hoot."

"Why?" asked Hushy.

"I don't know why. Now be quiet and go to sleep."

"Father dear, was that a hoot I made?"

"No, it was a noise, not a hoot."

"How come I can't hoot?"

"Because you have to learn," said his father. "It takes practice."

"Will I be able to hoot when I'm big like you?"

"Yes! You will be able to hoot," promised his father. "Now, please go to sleep."

"But I'm not tired; I don't feel the least bit sleepy."

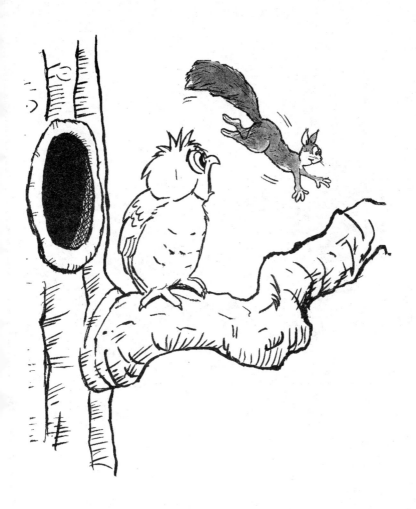

Hushy heard a noise high above him in the
trees. He looked up and a red furry animal
climbed down beside him.

"Mother!" He yelled loudly. "There is a big, red, furry thing with a bushy tail beside me."

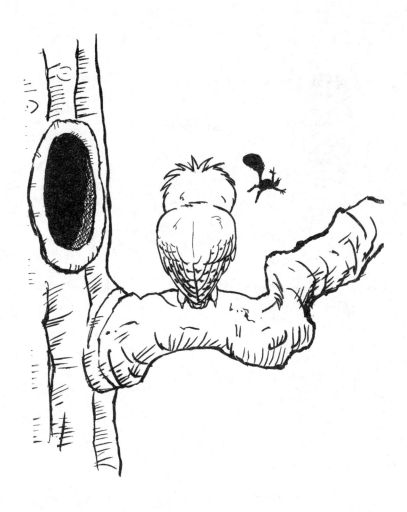

The squirrel jumped onto another branch
and hurried away.

"It's gone now, Mummy. But it was here, honest, and it wasn't a robin."

"How can anyone sleep with you asking so many questions?" snapped his mother.

"I was only curious, Mother dear."

"It was a red squirrel," yelled Coney, his big sister, who was cross about being wakened. Something moved below him. He looked down and saw a big, red, creature with a bushy tail.

"Mother, you are not going to believe me, but I see something big and red below the tree and it's not a robin, or a squirrel, and it has a white tip on its tail."

The animal looked up at Hushy. "I'm a fox!"
it said. Then it padded away.

"Mummy," the young owl yelled. "You don't have to tell me what it was. I know already! It said 'I'm a fox!' It didn't mean *I* was a fox, but that *it* was a fox. You see?"

A butterfly flitted about the trees, then
landed on Hushy's head.

"Mummy!" whispered Hushy. "Mum," he said a little louder, but there was still no answer. *"Ma!"* Hushy yelled loudly.

The red admiral flitted away.

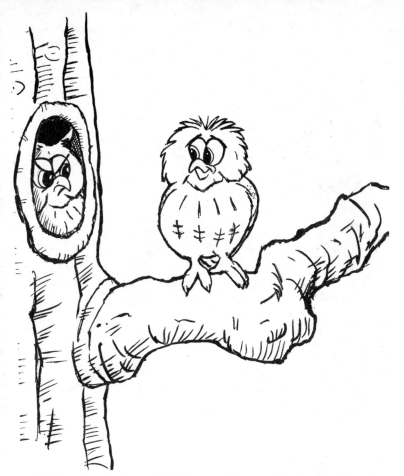

"What is it now?" his mother asked, looking very cross.

"I was about to show you something cute. It was very small and it had big wings, but not as big as mine, Mummy, and a teeny weeny body."

Then the butterfly flitted past again.

Hushy jumped up and down on the branch. "There it is, Mummy! I can see it again."

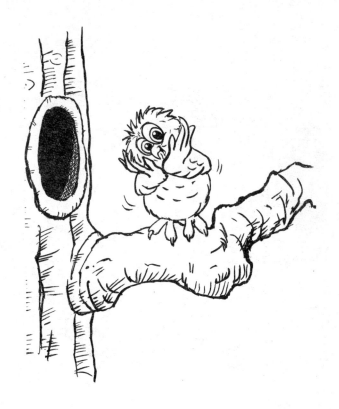

"That's a butterfly called a red admiral," said his mother. "Now, come inside and go to sleep."

"Mummy, how come owls sleep all day and stay up all night?" asked Hushy.

"That's just the way it is," said his mother in a very sleepy voice.

Hushy was about to go inside the tree when a spider crawled down its web in front of him.

He let out a loud shriek. "Mummy, Daddy, there's a monster out here with lots of legs. Help!"

Mummy and Daddy Owl peered out and saw
the spider. "That is nothing to be scared of," his
daddy chuckled. "It's only a little cross spider."

"I think it looks *very* cross," said Hushy trembling.

"No, dear, that's its name," said his mother. "It's because of the cross shape on its back. Don't worry, it won't hurt you."

His big sister, Coney, stuck her head out and laughed. "You big baby, afraid of a little spider!"

"I'm not a baby," snapped Hushy.

Hushy went inside and cuddled up close to
his mother. He was feeling very sleepy after
his busy day.

"Oh, look," said Coney. "The moon is awake! Mummy and Daddy, it's time to wake up."

Mummy and Daddy Owl stepped out onto the branch, followed by Coney.

"What a beautiful starry night," said Mummy Owl.

Daddy Owl called to Hushy. "Hushy! Hushy! It's time to wake up."

There was no answer.

"Wake up, Hushy!" yelled Coney. "It's night time, it's time to get up and practise your flying."

"Time to wake up, dear," said Mother. "There are lots of lovely things to see. Look at the beautiful stars."

"I'm too tired," yawned Hushy. "I want to go to sleep. I'll be an owl tomorrow night."